Custe

MITCHELL SHARMAT

HELLO...THIS IS MY FATHER SPEAKING

HarperCollinsPublishers

HELLO . . . THIS IS MY FATHER SPEAKING

Printed in the United States of America. For information address HarperCollins Children's Books, a division of HarperCollins Publishers, 10 East 53rd Street, New York, NY 10022.

Library of Congress Cataloging-in-Publication Data
Sharmat, Mitchell.
Hello—this is my father speaking / Mitchell Sharmat.
p. cm.
Summary: Embarrassed that his father cleans offices for a living, Jeff Whitty gets involved in the stock market, hoping to make enough money so that his father can quit his job.
ISBN 0-06-024469-0. — ISBN 0-06-024472-0 (lib. bdg.)
[1. Investments—Fiction. 2. Stock market—Fiction. 3. Fathers and sons—Fiction.] I. Title.
PZ7.S52992He 1994 93-50951
[Fic]—dc20 CIP
AC

Typography by Elynn Cohen
1 2 3 4 5 6 7 8 9 10
❖
First Edition

For Dudley,
who really knows how to grow hair
and
for Nathan,
who is off to a good start.
—M.S.

ONE

What a mess I've made of things! But nothing like the mess that's going to be here soon. It's rolling down the highway from Chicago and getting closer every second.

Once Mom and Dad find out, will they ever forgive me? Will I stop worrying that every strange car on the street carries an FBI agent coming to take me away? Will the lawn in front of our house recover from what's going to happen to it?

I want to run away and hide for a hundred years. Then I could come back when everyone has forgotten what I did. It's going to take that long.

No. I'd better sit here and wait and face the music. The funeral music.

—·—

It began innocently. I just wanted to help my father. Now I know I should have left well enough alone. Me and my big ideas.

It was about three months ago when my teacher, Ms. Kelly, said, "We're going to have Career Day later in the school year. Who'll volunteer to ask their parents to come by and talk to us?"

No one raised a hand.

Ms. Kelly continued, "Don't be shy. I've met your parents and I know many of them have interesting jobs."

Julie Samson raised her hand. Julie lives next door to me. "My mother is an account executive for an advertising agency."

Ms. Kelly made a note on her pad. "Thank you, Julie. Anyone else?"

Ms. Kelly started to walk down my aisle. I began to sweat and scrunched down in my seat. Don't look at me, I prayed.

She stopped at Albie Lear's desk. "Your father rents space for a national real estate broker, doesn't he?"

Albie turned red in the face. "Yes, ma'am," he stammered.

Ms. Kelly smiled. "Will you ask him to speak to us on Career Day?"

"Yes, ma'am," Albie said.

She wrote down Albie's name and started down the aisle again. I closed my eyes and tried to will her past me. I could hear her footsteps. They stopped. I opened my eyes. Ms. Kelly was standing next to me, but she was looking at Howie Coin. Howie had raised his hand. What a pal that Howie is, I thought.

"I volunteer to ask my father," Howie was saying. "He's a computer programmer."

Ms. Kelly checked her list. "Now let's see. We have a programmer, an advertising executive, and a commercial real estate broker. We need a small-business person."

She turned and looked directly at me. "Well, Jeff, what about your father? He owns his own business. He can tell us all about free enterprise and how to start and run a small business."

"Nothing's smaller than his business," I said. "He works out of his garage. All he talks about are his problems and worries. You wouldn't want to hear that."

I could hear everybody laughing and I felt more embarrassed than ever.

"Quiet, please," said Ms. Kelly, looking around. Then she put her hand on my shoulder. "The class should find that interesting. Please ask him."

"Yeah, pretty please!" shouted Albie as the bell rang. I started to lunge for him, but Ms. Kelly was in the way and he escaped.

Howie and I walked home after school. Howie lives two doors down from me on the other side of Julie Samson's house.

"You're going to ask your father to speak, aren't you?" Howie asked.

I shrugged. "I dunno. Cleaning offices is so . . . so boring."

"No more boring than what Mike does," said Howie.

Mike is Howie's father. Howie and his father are on a first-name basis. I'm also on a first-name basis with him.

I pushed Howie's head. "Come off it. Mike is really with it. Doesn't he design computer systems that control the operations of dozens of businesses?"

"Yeah, but it's still boring," said Howie. "You think computers and you think glamour. But all it is is detail work. Everything is numbers. No personality. No flowers. No shine. It's enough to drive anyone nuts."

"Mike's not nuts," I said. "He's a regular guy, a

pal. Joking around all the time."

Howie stopped walking. "Do you really think that what your father does is boring?"

Howie didn't give me a chance to answer. "Compared to what Mike does, your father's absolutely a creative genius. And he's creative every day."

"What do you mean?"

"Every day your dad creates a bright clean environment for people to work in. In my book that's more important than neat columns of figures."

"Okay, okay," I said. "I don't think it's boring. That was just an excuse. What I can't stand about my father's business is that it's turned him into a Mr. Sanitary Master cartoon. It's that cleaning franchise that Dad bought into, with their stupid gimmicks. Ever seen my father's work uniform? It's got a T-shirt with a picture of Mr. Sanitary Master. Mr. Sanitary Master wears a cape made of a gigantic dust rag! And he's wearing tights and a mask. And he's got a motto under his feet: I'M MR. SANITARY MASTER. MY MISSION: CONQUER DUST, BANISH BACTERIA, ZAP DIRT. And there's even a company chant: 'Fungus is the foe, germs gotta go, blah, blah, blah.'"

I groaned. "If my dad ever came to class

wearing that T-shirt and chanting . . ."

Howie laughed. "I think it's kind of funny. But anyway, your dad's a neat guy. Just ask him not to show up in the T-shirt on Career Day."

Howie started to walk again. "Problem solved."

"No, it isn't. You've seen his van. Mr. Sanitary Master is standing life-size in glowing colors on both sides. When Dad drives up to school in that . . ."

"Plenty of kids have seen it already," Howie said.

"Yeah, but now they'll pay attention to it and *me.* I can just hear the razzing."

"Okay, I get it. So your dad's cleaning business is fine with you, but . . ."

"Right. Why does he have to be a comic book character while he does it?" I said.

"Does your dad know how you feel?" Howie asked.

"Well, I asked him to dump his Mr. Sanitary Master image. But he says that's his business identification."

"The way he's going, maybe he'll make so much money that you'll get rich and he can quit or send someone else out wearing the T-shirt."

"Dream on, Howie."

Howie closed his eyes and pretended to snore.

Then he opened his eyes and said, "Well, here we are at my house already. Forget fathers. Come on in and let's raid the refrigerator."

"Thanks, but no thanks."

I had some thinking to do. Especially about Career Day.

But when I got home, I found that my life had changed. There was a note addressed to me on the kitchen counter. It said:

Dear Jeff,

Terri and I have gone out to Troutberg. Grandmother is sick, so we'll be staying with her until she gets better. I've spoken to Dad and he says he'll take care of you. You know how busy he is, so be a good boy and do what he says and try not to get into trouble. I'll call soon.

Love,
Mom

TWO

My father wasn't always a Mr. Sanitary Master cleaner working out of his garage. He used to be an engineer in the design lab of a major defense contractor.

My dad had had an important job. He was in charge of the secret calculations controlling the trajectory of one of the intercontinental ballistic missile systems. When the cold war ended and the budget crunch came, his program was canceled and he was laid off. He spent a whole year looking around for another engineering job, but because his work was so specialized, he had no luck.

One day he was listening to Henry Martin on the radio. Henry is Dad's favorite news commentator. Anyhow, Henry was advertising Mr. Sanitary Master.

"Now friends," Henry Martin said, "I want to talk to you about one of the fastest-growing companies in America, Mr. Sanitary Master. Remember that name, Mr. Sanitary Master. Mr. Sanitary Master offers the most modern, the most efficient, the most scientific space-age cleaning system on the face of the earth. Whether it be a one-car garage or a hundred-story office building, Mr. Sanitary Master will do your cleaning job faster, cleaner, and more cost effectively.

"And do you know what else? We're growing so fast, we may have room for *you* in the Mr. Sanitary Master family. Call us today, and tonight you'll get down on your knees and thank me. I promise you will. If you want financial independence such as you never dreamed of, call us at 1-800-555-1717. And when you hear why we're called Mr. Sanitary Master, I just know you'll want to join our family of franchised dealers.

"We'll be with you every step of the way to financial independence. Don't just take my word for it. Ask John Gorman of Oklahoma City, Oklahoma, or Abe Horblit of Chicago, Illinois.

They called, and are they glad they did! That number again, 1-800-555-1717. Call today. Tonight talk our proposition over with your spouse. Then I know you will be one of us. God bless you and good day."

That night Dad told us what Henry Martin had said. Dad is a great believer in family decisions. He says the family is the basis of democracy, and Dad's a great believer in democracy. But have you ever noticed that the families with the most financial problems are the ones that have the most family discussions? I bet millionaires don't have democratic debates about how the family money is spent. All I know is the longer Dad was out of work, the more family discussions we had.

Mom said Dad should look into Mr. Sanitary Master. "It doesn't look like the defense industry will be rehiring soon."

Dad winced. "If and when they do," he said, "I may find that I'm obsolete."

Dad went over to the telephone and called 1-800-555-1717. He spoke for a while. Then he gave his name, address, and telephone number, said thank you, and hung up.

A few days later a large envelope arrived from Mr. Sanitary Master. It contained a brochure, an application blank, a cleaning supplies catalog, a sample contract, a sheet of testimonials, and a picture of Henry Martin on a letter of greeting.

Dad looked over the material and showed it to Mom.

After she read it, Mom said, "They want $5,000. If you really think you'd like to try, it's all right with me. But be sure it's what you want to do. Once you've made the investment, you've got to see it through to the end. It's a real commitment."

Dad ran his fingers through his hair. "Well, I've always liked to work with my hands. I'll have plenty of chances to do that, at least at the start. Later, if the business grows, I'll be more into management. Besides, if it doesn't work out, the $5,000 won't all be thrown away. We get a power vacuum, a mechanical floor washer, and a power buffer. Plus a starter set of the most advanced cleaning supplies and hand tools on the market today."

Did you notice that no one asked me or my sister, Terri, what we thought? So much for family democracy.

Dad filled out the application blank and mailed it with a check for $5,000 to Mr. Sanitary Master. Two weeks later he received a letter welcoming him to the Mr. Sanitary Master family.

The letter said that his initial order of supplies and equipment was already on its way to him. He was also invited to attend the next weeklong session of Building Cleaning College in Abilene, Texas.

That afternoon Transway Freight Forwarders left five large boxes in our driveway. One contained the power vac and attachments. Another, the floor scrubber. Another held the polisher. The fourth had cleaning supplies and tools. The fifth, and biggest, contained assorted sizes and colors of cleaning rags with the initials M.S.M. embossed on each of them.

So far, so good. But then, tucked away with the rags in its own little packet were two dozen T-shirts with you-know-who's picture and motto emblazoned across the front. And there was other Mr. Sanitary Master stuff. Decals of him. Small, medium, and large. Stencils. And directions for putting Mr. Sanitary Master in all his caped and masked germ-free glory across the sides of a van.

Yuck!

"Dad, can we just toss this stuff away?" I asked. "The world already has Superman, Batman, Spiderman, the Lone Ranger . . . it doesn't need a Mr. Sanitary Master."

What I meant was *I* didn't need a Mr. Sanitary

Master for a father!

My father was holding up a T-shirt. "Jeff," he said, "Mr. Sanitary Master is a logo, an identification. I need it. It's a meaningful part of the franchise I bought."

"You mean you forked over $5,000 to become a masked man in tights wearing a dust-cloth cape?"

My father smiled patiently. "Jeff, most of the money obviously went into the large items—the tools of the trade, so to speak. But, yes, some of it went for the privilege of becoming Mr. Sanitary Master. I'm the only one in town. I bought the territory. This is my cleaning turf."

My father posed, flexing his muscles. There was nothing more that I, Jeff Whitty, now a.k.a. the son of San, could say. I watched my father standing there, with all his new equipment and stuff around him. He looked so enthusiastic about taking a chance, starting something new. I had an urge to help him, to hug him, to hug him into success. But I was getting too old for that kind of stuff.

Instead, I helped Dad clean out the garage and build racks and bins to hold the equipment and supplies for the world's newest Mr. Sanitary Master.

From then on our car had to be parked outside in the driveway. Our garage now belonged to Mr. Sanitary Master.

We all pitched in to help Dad get started, even Terri. She's much younger than I am—she's in kindergarten—and she's always covered with dripping chocolate. A lousy advertisement for our cleaning service. Well, Mr. Sanitary Master doesn't clean children or dogs or anything like that.

Things started out slowly. Dad had some flyers printed offering to clean houses and stores and offices at a very low price considering he was going to clean them with space-age technology. Terri, Dad, and I went out and papered the area for a half mile around our home. Mom stayed home to answer the telephone.

The first week Dad got five calls to clean houses. Sounds terrific, doesn't it? But remember, Mr. Sanitary Master can't just go over and clean a house. First he has to have a consultation with the owners. Then he has to give them a written estimate. Such a big deal!

And there's the contract. A space-age cleaning service has to do everything under a contract. But homeowners aren't used to signing contracts to get their figurines dusted and toilets scrubbed.

So you can see it took a little while for Dad to get enough customers who were willing to sign contracts and give him repeat business. But slowly it did happen.

Then Dad figured it was time to expand. He bought space on every other bus bench in our area. Business picked up so fast, Dad had to hire two guys to help him.

Then Dad got his big break. The new edition of the Yellow Pages came out, and Dad's Mr. Sanitary Master ad was in it. Unlike the bench ads, this one had a picture of Mr. Sanitary Master in it. Fortunately my friends don't read the Yellow Pages. Anyway, I never would have guessed that Mr. Sanitary Master would have such credibility or recognition value. People would call up and say, "Mr. Sanitary Master, I saw your ad in the Yellow Pages." As if he were a real person. Now these calls weren't from beleaguered homemakers. These calls were from established businesses looking for what Dad referred to as "stability in their cleaning contractor." And I guess they also liked to think that their wastepaper baskets were going to be emptied in the most advanced manner possible.

Many of these customers wanted their places cleaned at night, so Dad's business became an eighteen-hours-a-day affair. He now had one foreman and eight helpers. And a secondhand van with a huge Mr. Sanitary Master complete with motto on both sides.

This meant that we now had a car *and* a secondhand van parked in our driveway. Julie Samson's mother complained that our driveway looked like a used-car lot and was dragging the neighborhood down.

She didn't understand. Dad was doing the best he could.

But I cringed every time I saw that caped crusader against dirt leering down at me in my driveway.

THREE

With Mom and Terri away, I thought I was going to have a blast. I'd have the whole house to myself most of the time. Do whatever I wanted. But Dad was on to me.

Right from the start he decided that I shouldn't be left at home alone while he went on his night jobs.

"Why?" I asked.

"Because," he answered.

"You think I'm going to get into trouble, don't you?"

"No."

"You don't trust me."

"Sure I do. You're a good boy, but you're so full of ideas. I'd feel better if you came with me. I'll pick you up at suppertime and we'll grab a bite to eat. Then we'll go on to my evening cleaning jobs. Bring your homework along. We'll find a place for you to do it. And don't make such a face."

That first night Dad picked me up at five thirty. We stopped off to have pizza.

"This is a good idea," I said. "Hey, we're going to have some fun after all while Mom's out of town."

"Not too much fun." He smiled. "We both have our work to do."

"I'd rather do my work at home. I do much better with the stereo on."

We wolfed down one large pizza with three toppings. Then Dad said, "Let's go. We're late."

We left the pizza parlor and drove to the offices of Star Crossed Securities.

This was a regular five-nights-a-week job for Dad. Star Crossed Securities is a national stockbrokerage company with local offices coast to coast. Their motto is "The heavens shine on our investments." Maybe you've seen their commercials on TV with people having a good time counting and spending money under a sky full of stars.

Anyhow, this company is so big that even my dad had felt sure enough about them to open an investment account there, even before he got the cleaning contract for their local office. He had bought what he called a few safe stocks that paid dividends.

When we got to the office, Dad's cleaning crew was already at work. Dad told me to wait while he saw how everything was going.

I stood at the entrance. The place was huge! It was one tremendous room with about fifty open cubicles. Each cubicle had a desk and two chairs in it. Along the walls of this monster room were larger cubicles, each enclosed by glass that ran from the floor to the ceiling.

When Dad returned, he said, "Find a clean desk to work at, and don't touch any papers. You can never tell what might be important in an investment office."

I looked around for a clean desk. Most of them had papers strewn and piled all over them. Then I noticed a nice clean desk in one of the glass-enclosed cubicles. I headed for it.

Just as I was about to lay my stuff down on the desk, Dad stopped me.

"Hold it, Jeff," he said. "This is the branch manager's office. You'd better find another place to work."

You can't imagine what slobs these stockbrokers are. Most of them keep their cubicles like I keep my room at home. I finally found a desk with a lot of papers neatly stacked. Most of the desk was clean. A sign on the cubicle said that this desk belonged to Patricia Davis.

It took me less than an hour to do all my homework. I don't know why some kids make such a fuss over doing homework. Once you get to it, it doesn't take too long. An hour, maybe two tops.

I got up and looked for Dad. I found him polishing the handles on the entrance door.

"I'm through," I said.

"With what?"

"My homework, of course."

Dad then said what he always says. "Through already? When I was a boy, I always had four hours of homework a night and more on weekends."

"I know! I know! So, is there anything I can do?"

"Okay, why don't you look around and see if you can find something the crew might have missed."

I looked around a bit, but didn't see anything that wasn't taken care of until I got back to

Patricia Davis's desk. A sheet of paper had gotten wedged in her wastebasket and hadn't come out when they emptied it. I pulled it out and started playing tic tac toe with myself. Dumb game. I won every time. I began yawning.

I turned the paper over and read what was printed on the other side. It was some kind of list called Fundamental Recommendations. On the list was the name Dudley Labs, and a penciled note that the FDA had approved a Dudley drug—Bald-Away—for use in treating male baldness.

I looked at the list for a minute. I scratched my head. I've got plenty of hair, I thought. I threw the paper back into the basket. "What a bore!"

Then I thought, Wait a minute. I fished the paper back out of the basket and looked at it again. What did the recommendation really mean? I decided to ask Dad. I looked for him, but he wasn't in sight.

I got up and wandered around the office. This was some place. I bet that none of the stockbrokers had to wear a stupid T-shirt in order to work here. And nobody drove to work with a caped masked man as a painted passenger on the outside.

I finally found Dad in the ladies' room cleaning the mirror. I showed him my piece of paper. "What does this stuff mean?" I asked.

"It looks like tic tac toe to me."

"No, Dad, not that." I turned the paper over. "I mean this recommendation stuff about Dudley and male baldness."

"Oh, *that*," he said. "I don't know. The only investment I've made in the stock market since I got into the cleaning business is soap companies. I figure it's best to stick with what I know best, and right now that's cleaning supplies."

I looked at Dad to see if he was putting me on, and decided that he wasn't. I also saw that he was beginning to lose his hair. Funny, I hadn't noticed that before.

I put the paper in my pocket. I didn't know what I was going to do with it, but something made me take it with me when we left Star Crossed Securities.

As Dad locked the door, I took a last look back inside. Yes. This was some place to work, all right. There was something awesome going on here. I could smell it. Suddenly, I knew I wanted to get in on the action.

FOUR

The next morning I started out for school.

"Where've you been?" Howie shouted as he came running down the steps from his house.

If you haven't guessed it already, Howie and I walk to school together almost every day.

Howie caught up with me. "I called you last night, but there wasn't any answer."

"I wasn't home," I told him. "Dad took me out to eat, and then I went with him on his job at Star Crossed Securities."

"Who are they?" Howie asked.

"Stockbrokers. And look what I found there." I

pulled out the recommendation on Dudley and showed it to Howie.

"What's the big deal?" he said. "Afraid you're going bald? Looking for a new hair cream?"

I patted my hair into place. "No, nothing like that."

"Then what?"

"I'm not sure, but I may be on to something big."

"You mean male baldness? I hear there's a lot of it going around. Hey, a drug that grows hair? Now that should be a real growth industry."

"Ha, ha, Howie," I said. "This may be an opportunity. I've got a feeling that I'm going to get a really big idea."

"Oh no, not again," moaned Howie. "This time count me out. I haven't recovered from your last big idea."

"Don't worry," I said. "I've learned my lesson. I'll be very careful. I'll go one step at a time."

But even as I spoke, I was getting excited. I was getting so excited I couldn't stand it, and I didn't even know what my idea was—yet.

At school, Ms. Kelly started to talk about careers again. She said that we should investigate different careers so that we could make good class choices in high school. The minute she said *investigate,* I knew it was fate.

I decided on the spot that that afternoon I would go down and talk to the people at Star Crossed Securities.

—·—

When I walked in the door of Star Crossed Securities, the place looked different. There were men and women everywhere. Some were in the cubicles talking on the phone or watching video monitors. Others were rushing up and down the aisles carrying pieces of paper.

A woman sitting up front was busy answering one telephone call after another. I must have looked lost, because she smiled and waved me over. "Are you looking for someone?" she asked.

"Dudley!" I blurted out.

She thought a moment, smiled again. "We don't have anyone named Dudley here. We have several Dougs, but no Dudleys. Are you sure you're in the right place?"

"No, you don't understand," I said. "I want to find out about a company whose name is Dudley."

"Do you have a regular broker?" she asked.

I shook my head no. This was beginning to get sticky, and I didn't know what to say next. But the woman was trying hard to be helpful.

She looked at a list on her desk. "Wait," she said. "I'll try to get someone to help you."

She dialed a number and spoke into her phone. "Harold, you're the broker of the day, aren't you? Good. I've got a young man here at the front desk. He has some questions about a company called Dudley. Can you help him?"

She looked at me and said, "What is your name, sir?"

I told her.

Then she spoke to this Harold on the phone again and said, "His name is Jeff Whitty. Yes. I'll tell him to wait."

The lady hung up and smiled again. "Have a seat. Mr. Goodbody will be out in a few minutes."

I took a seat in the waiting area. People were coming in and out all the time, and the lady said hello and good-bye to all of them, that is, when she wasn't too busy answering the phone. She called almost all of them by name.

After five minutes a man dressed in a light tan suit came out. He must have been at least 25 years old. He looked around and called out, "Mr. Whitty?"

The second he said my name, my heart started to pound and I felt a hot flush come over my face. I don't know why I got so agitated. I had come there of my own free will. But I felt like I'd been hauled before some judge for some alleged crime. And I wasn't even planning a crime.

I stood up. "That's me."

The man looked at me awkwardly for a split second. I guess he didn't expect me to be as young as I was. Then he put his hand out to shake mine. "Harold Goodbody. Come with me."

He led the way back to his cubicle and offered me a seat.

When we both had sat down, he asked, "What can I do for you?"

"I'm interested in Dudley Labs."

"What would you like to know?"

"Is it a good investment?"

"It might be," he said. "It all depends on what else you own and how it fits into your portfolio."

Of course I didn't have a portfolio. I didn't even own one stock, but I kept my cool. "Yeah. Right," I said.

"How much money do you have to invest?" Mr. Goodbody asked.

I thought he was beginning to catch on to me. I only wondered what had taken him so long.

"Not much," I admitted.

"Too bad," he said. "Let's see, have you ever thought about mutual funds?"

"Thought about them? I never heard of them."

His face lit up. It was like he had a chance to pitch the one thing he knew.

"They're perfect for the beginning investor with only a little money," he said. "What you do is buy into a mutual fund, and they in turn invest your money along with that of a lot of other investors in a basketful of stocks. With the risk spread over many stocks, you can't get hurt too much, and you get professional management to boot."

Mr. Goodbody reached into a drawer and pulled out a couple of brochures. "Here, take these home and have your parents read them. If they're interested, have them call me. My name and number are stamped on the brochures."

I was getting nowhere fast. I had come down to Star Crossed Securities to find out about careers and Dudley and how the business operated. Now all I had to show for my efforts was a fistful of brochures about some dull mutual-funds companies.

I was feeling discouraged. Then I felt this strong hand on my shoulder. I looked up. I saw a short roly-poly man wearing horn-rimmed glasses.

"I see you have a new client, Harold," the short

man said to Mr. Goodbody.

Harold Goodbody forced a smile.

The short man went on, "Well, Kid, Ginnie at the front desk tells me you're interested in Dudley. Did Harold here tell you what you wanted to know?"

"No sir. Not yet, anyhow. He's been telling me about mutual funds."

"I see," said the short man. "Are you almost through?" he asked Harold.

"We were just winding down, Sid," said Mr. Goodbody.

"Good," said the man whom Mr. Goodbody called Sid. "Kid, come with me and we'll chew the fat. I'm Sid Balzac. I'm one of the assistant managers."

"Glad to meet you, Mr. Balzac," I said.

"Call me Sid," he said.

"You can call me Jeff," I said.

"Nah," said Sid. "I'll call you Kid." And he rumpled my hair.

Sid Balzac took me to his office. It was one of the glass cubicles along the walls. His was bigger than most of the others. He sat down behind his desk and lit a big cigar.

"Squat," he said.

I sat down in one of the chairs opposite him.

He punched a few keys on the keyboard connected to his computer, took a puff on his cigar, thought about something for a minute, and then relaxed.

He turned and looked at me intently. "Well, Kid, what's your interest in Dudley?"

I looked at his balding head and didn't know

if I should mention that they'd found a treatment for baldness. So I decided to start at the beginning and tell him what had brought me there.

"My father owns a cleaning service that cleans these offices every night," I told him.

"That's Whitty's Mr. Sanitary Master, isn't it?"

"Yes, sir."

"And so you're Jeff Whitty. Right?"

"Right."

"Okay, Kid, go on."

"Well, we're going to have a Career Day at school. I was asked to bring my father to talk to our class about what it's like to run his own business. Well, that would be great, except for . . ."

"For what, Kid?"

I squirmed in my chair. "My dad has become a cartoon character. It's part of his cleaning franchise identity."

I sat up. "You don't have a Mr. Star Crossed Securities Man here, do you? You don't have to drive a van with a caped figure on it or wear a dumb T-shirt or anything like that, do you?"

"Not that I've noticed, Kid."

I kept talking. "Well, Dad brought me on his job here last night, and this looked like a great place to work. I mean in the daytime, at a desk, without a T-shirt."

Sid flicked his cigar ash toward his ashtray, but missed.

"Let me see if I follow this," he said. "You want your father to quit what he's doing and work here?"

"Well, I'm not sure. I'm proud of the way he's building his business, but I just want him to be Mr. Tony Whitty, not Mr. Sanitary Master. And I got such vibes about this place last night. For openers, that Dudley thing."

Sid wiped the ashes from his desk. Then he puffed again on his cigar and let out a big cloud of smoke. "Ah, Dudley. You're ready to talk Dudley? Go on."

I reached into my pocket and pulled out the recommendation on Dudley. "I . . . uh . . . found this in one of your wastebaskets last night," I said.

My hand was shaking as I gave the paper to Sid.

SIX

Don't pay any attention to the tic tac toes," I said as I stuffed the piece of paper into Sid's hand.

Sid raised an eyebrow. "Exactly what do you see in Dudley?"

I started to get enthusiastic. I even forgot about Sid's balding head. "It's the male-baldness bit. I thought there was something to it. I showed the recommendation to my friend Howie. And like that he says, There's a lot of it—male baldness, that is—going around these days. So I figured that a company that might be coming up with a cure could make a fortune."

"Is your friend Howie also interested in the stock market?"

"Nah! I just figured if even Howie can see a connection between male baldness and a drug-maker, there must be something to it."

"And what does your father think about it?"

"He says now the only thing he invests in is soaps. He says you should invest in what you know best. Since he's in the cleaning business, he thinks he understands soaps best."

"I see. Do you think he's right?"

I shrugged.

Sid punched a few keys on his keyboard. "Kid, come over here to this side of the desk. I want to show you something." He pointed to the monitor with his cigar.

I went around and saw:

DUD Dudley Technical Recommendation. Support 100. Resistance 112. Buy near 102 target 108. Stop 99 1/8.

I keep looking at the monitor. "What does it mean?" I asked.

"The current price of Dudley is 105. But see here on the monitor. The recommendation is that it should be bought near 102 and sold at 108.

"Let's say you wait for the price of Dudley to go

down from 105 to 102. Then you buy 100 shares at 102. That will cost you $10,200. Now you wait and watch for the price to go up to the 108 target price. Then you sell your 100 shares at 108 and you get $10,800, and that means you get a profit of . . ."

I thought fast. "That's $600," I blurted out. "But that's only 6 percent. I can do about as good in a bank."

"Yeah, in a year you could. But if you could do it in two weeks, what would you think of $600 then?"

"Let's see. That's $600 divided by $10,200 times 52 divided by 2. That would be . . . My God, that would be 150 percent. Can *that* be right?"

"Good figuring, Kid. That's the way the numbers work out."

"But that's got to be stealing. No one makes money like that."

Sid laughed. "We don't do it every time, but if we do it more than 50 percent of the time, we're ahead of the game."

"Hey, that's neat!" I laughed. "But what's all this got to do with male baldness?"

"Someday that Dudley baldness drug, Bald-Away, may mean a lot to the earnings of Dudley. But that day is a long way off. A bottle of

Bald-Away costs $135 at the drugstore. That's for a month's supply. One hundred thirty-five a month for hair treatments is just too many bucks. At that price it can't be a mass-market item. If they can get the costs way down, that's another story."

"So that means that Bald-Away is a dud for Dudley right now?" I asked. I hoped he liked my little joke.

"Wrong," he said. "Right now there are enough jokers out there who believe that any company that can grow hair can grow money, and so, even though Dudley stock might go down, it won't go down much."

"Meaning?"

"Meaning I'd feel safe making the short-term trade . . . the recommendation we've just been looking at on the monitor."

My head was spinning. This was complicated.

Just then an old man popped his head into the office. He was excited. "Sid, did you see that Marvel just hit 35? I think we ought to sell!"

Sid punched up MRV and checked his monitor. "Right on the mark, Vinnie!" he said.

Vinnie left and Sid flew into action. He grabbed a pen and some small forms and started writing. When he finished, he dashed out of the room with the forms. He was gone about five minutes.

When Sid returned, he was smiling and shaking his head. "Vinnie just made $10,000 in two days. That guy knows how to trade. You can learn a lot from a customer like him, even though he was a jewelry salesman until he retired."

"Here." Sid gave me a piece of paper he had in his hand. It was a printout of the Dudley recommendation we had seen on the screen. "Take this home with you, and watch the action of Dudley in the financial pages of the newspaper."

"How do I do that?"

Sid turned around and took a newspaper from the table behind him. He opened it to the stock-market tables in the back section and motioned for me to come look at it.

"Look." He pointed to the top of the page. "See these three columns? They show the high, low, and closing prices of the day for each of the stocks on the page."

I watched Sid move his finger down the page. "All the stocks are listed in alphabetical order," he said.

His finger stopped. "Now see this horizontal line of print?"

I nodded yes.

"Good. What does it say?"

"It says Dudly, and then there's a number in its high column, in its low column, and in its close column. Did they spell Dudley wrong?"

"That's their shorthand for Dudley. They don't have enough room to spell all the names in full, so they make up abbreviations. They start by leaving out some or all of the vowels."

"I get it," I said. "I'll be able to read what the highest price, the lowest price, and the closing price for Dudley is each day."

"Good," Sid said. "Just watch the price action of Dudley every day in the paper. It'll give you a better idea of this business than reading a hundred books."

I put the printout Sid had given me in my pocket.

Sid walked me to the door. "Keep in touch, Kid," he said. "If you have any questions, come on in and we'll talk. You've a good head for figures. I've got a hunch you'd be a natural in this business."

He patted me on the shoulder, and I was out the door.

What a blast! Vinnie had made $10,000 on Marvel in two days. Let's see, the return on investing in Dudley could be 150 percent. If Dad and I invested $10,000 and made 150 percent on it, in a year we'd have a $15,000 profit plus the original $10,000. That would be $25,000. This was the big time! Our money could grow faster than the new hair springing up on bald heads all over the country. We could get rich fast, and maybe Dad wouldn't have to be Mr. Sanitary Master anymore. And Sid thought I'd be a natural in this business.

Now if I could only get my hands on $10,000.

SEVEN

I sat down and made a list of people I knew who might be able to scrape up $10,000. It was a very short list. Dad was the only one on it. But if he could take a long shot on something as risky as Mr. Sanitary Master, why couldn't he be interested in as sure a thing as trading Dudley between 102 and 108?

I told Dad about my visit with Sid Balzac. I left out the part where I talked to Sid about my problem with Mr. Sanitary Master and went right into how Vinnie had made $10,000 in two days. And I told Dad how he could turn 6 percent into 150 percent. I watched his face as I explained what I wanted him to do, and I thought he was getting interested.

Then I finished up, “All you need is $10,000 to get started.”

“Me? I’m already invested in the stock market. Soap companies. I told you. Nice, clean, nothing fancy. No big ups or downs. I don’t have to pay attention to them. I just let the stocks sit and they pay a nice, clean dividend.”

My father chuckled. “You know what I call your idea? Hair today, and gone tomorrow.”

Then he walked over to his bookcase and pulled out a story by some Russian about a gambler. He made me sit down and read it.

I didn’t read every word. I thought the whole thing was a downer. If you ask me, all Russian writers are downers. Anyhow, the point of the story was that you shouldn’t gamble what you have to live on for the sake of the extras in life.

I didn’t see how this story applied to me, and I told Dad so. I could see he was getting mad, but he bit his tongue and said it applied to him. That he had taken enough of a chance investing in Mr. Sanitary Master and he’d build his future one brick at a time.

I tried to argue with him that Dudley was almost a sure thing.

Then I went too far. I told him he wasn't building his future one brick at a time. He was building it one embossed cleaning rag at a time.

At that point he threatened to ground me and warned me not to bring up the $10,000 again. I figured he wasn't ready to listen to reason, so I backed off. That's what you have to do with adults. Sometimes they're with it and sometimes they're not. You've got to hit them at the right time.

Since I didn't have anything else to do just then, I started thinking about the gambler in the story. I could see he was wrong to bet his last dollar, or ruble, or whatever it was. After all, I'm not stupid. But he wasn't the only one in the story. There was this old lady. A countess or something. She won at cards. And that's how I got my next idea.

I thought about old ladies who might have $10,000 to spare. There was my grandma, but I had to rule her out. She was sick, and my mom probably wouldn't have let me get to her anyhow.

That left Julie Samson's mother. She was loaded. She even bought Julie an emerald ring for her twelfth birthday. Of course she isn't really old, but she's got a good start on getting there.

I felt a little funny thinking about going over

and asking her for the money. Now don't get me wrong. It wasn't the $10,000 that bothered me. It was just going over and talking to her about anything, since I knew she was mad that our car and van were cluttering our driveway. But when I really thought about *that,* I knew in my heart of hearts she was the right person to ask.

—·—

The next day Ms. Kelly gave us a current-events assignment. It was really African geography, but the way countries all over the world seem to keep changing their names and leaders, geography becomes current events. Our assignment was: Learn the names of all the African countries, their capitals, and their leaders. This wasn't a research project or anything like that. Ms. Kelly handed us sheets with all the information on it. It was straight drill.

After class, Howie walked out of the classroom with me.

"How about memorizing those crazy names together after school?" he asked.

"I don't know," I said. "I was thinking of asking Julie to help me with them."

Howie looked hurt. So I told him all about my visit with Sid Balzac and about Vinnie, and my conversation with Dad, and the idea I had of asking Mrs. Samson to put up $10,000.

Howie was stunned.

"This has to be the biggest stunt you've tried yet," he said. "I think you're getting in way over your head."

"I'm not getting anywhere unless I get $10,000," I said. "You don't happen to have $10,000, do you?"

Howie turned his pocket inside out. "Will $1.57 help?" he offered. "I guess not," he said. "Okay, you'll have to go ahead and hit on Mrs. Samson. Can I watch?"

I thought a minute. I wasn't sure it was such a good idea. I might get the money from Mrs. Samson if I spoke to her alone. But if Howie were there, it could get sticky.

"I don't know," I said.

"I'll tell you what," Howie said. "I'll tag along, and if things aren't going smoothly, I'll duck out."

What could I say? He had me. After all, he was my best friend. "Okay, you're on," I said.

After school we caught up with Julie.

"Hi," I said. "How would you like to do the African assignment together tonight?"

Julie hesitated. "I thought you did your homework with Howie," she said.

I had a brief moment of panic. Julie was going to put me off. I could see the $10,000 fading into the sunset.

But then my pal Howie saved the day. He said, "We thought we'd include you in."

Julie blushed and turned toward Howie with a big grin. "I'd love to," she said. "Why don't you drop by after supper? Say seven o'clock."

I would never have guessed it. Julie had a thing for Howie.

Dad said I could go to Julie's. I guess he didn't want me back at Star Crossed Securities. So at seven o'clock Howie and I were at Julie's. Julie opened the door. She had changed the ribbon in her hair. She led us back into the kitchen.

Mrs. Samson was there finishing the after-supper cleanup. "You kids can study at the table," she said.

We sat down and opened our books while Mrs. Samson went into the family room.

The Samson house is modeled after a farm-house. The family room is behind the kitchen, and a glass partition separates the two rooms. If you're in the kitchen you can see what's going on in the family room and vice versa, but you can't hear everything all that well—a pretty neat arrangement.

I watched as Mrs. Samson went over to a desk and started to work on some papers. I got busy working on the assignment with Howie and Julie. We got it licked in about an hour.

Then we started talking about other things. Actually, Howie and Julie were doing most of the talking. I looked into the family room and saw that Julie's mother was watching us. I smiled at her and she smiled back. That had to be a good sign.

I got up and went into the family room. I squeezed Howie's shoulder as I went by him. He looked up and gave me a wink.

I went over to Mrs. Samson. "Hi," I said.

"Hi yourself," she answered. "Have you finished?"

"Just about," I said. "Julie and Howie got to talking, so I decided I'd come over and talk to you."

"Oh?" Mrs. Samson looked surprised, but she also looked flattered.

I sat down across from her. "Do you know anything about the stock market?" I asked.

"A little," she said. "We have a modest portfolio."

"Do you invest or trade?" I asked.

"We invest," she said. "Why?"

"Well, it just so happens that I've been

spending some time at Star Crossed Securities and I spoke to a couple of men there."

"And?"

"One of them showed me how I could turn a quick 6 percent gain on a stock into a 150 percent gain within one year." I tried to read Mrs. Samson's face as she frowned.

"How do you do that?" she asked.

"By trading the stock in a well-defined range," I said triumphantly.

Mrs. Samson looked at me thoughtfully. "That doesn't work for most people," she said. "They can't stay on top of it."

"I can," I said. "I can with the help of my broker, Sid Balzac. All I need is $10,000. And if I can do it, I'll have enough money for lots of things. For example, I could afford to expand our garage, and my dad wouldn't have to keep the car and van in the driveway anymore. Are you interested?"

Mrs. Samson started to laugh. I could feel my ears turn red.

"You're making me an offer that's hard to refuse," she said.

Mrs. Samson laughed so hard that tears started to roll down her face. I usually can be counted on to say something, but when I get embarrassed, I never know what to say. So she kept laughing and I just sat there trying to pull myself together.

At last she stopped. "I think you have the germ of a good idea there. But it's too ambitious. Stick with investments and leave the trading alone, at least until you have more experience."

"How can I make enough that way?" I asked. "I don't have any money anyhow."

"I've an idea," she said.

I know when I get an idea it's bad enough. But when adults start getting ideas about your ideas, watch out.

"Have you thought about starting an investment club?"

"A what?" I couldn't figure out where she was headed.

"An investment club for kids," she said earnestly. "I think it would be terrific. To get it started, I'm willing to put up $1,000 for Julie. Then you'll only need another $9,000. You can sell units in $500 denominations. That way you'll only need another eighteen members at most."

Mrs. Samson was warming up to her pitch. She started talking about research committees and general meetings and keeping books and making reports and bylaws and everybody getting an education. What had started out being a simple request for $10,000 was turning into a nightmare.

I stood up and shook hands with Mrs. Samson. "I'll think about it," I told her.

I looked into the kitchen. I could see Howie smiling. He gave me the "way to go" sign. Little did he know how far I still had to go.

EIGHT

Julie saw us to the door.

"We'll have to do this again," she said.

"You bet!" Howie answered.

I just sort of grunted. I was disappointed and could do without *this again* for the rest of my life.

"Hey! What's with you?" Howie exclaimed as we walked down Julie's steps.

We stopped at the sidewalk. "I didn't get the $10,000," I said.

Howie looked puzzled. "From where I stood, it looked like you were hitting it off pretty well. I saw you shaking Mrs. Samson's hand and you both were smiling."

"Don't believe everything you see," I said. I put my arm around Howie's shoulder and started walking him toward his house. "I only got one thousand, with a million strings attached. Mrs. Samson wants to make an educational experience out of my idea. She wants us to start an investment club for kids."

We reached Howie's house and sat down on his steps.

"Maybe I'm missing something," he said, "but if I could get a thousand out of somebody's mother by just talking to her and shaking her hand, I'd be walking on air."

"I know what you mean," I said. "but one thou isn't enough to operate with. And I won't be able to move fast enough if I have to wait for meetings and committees and that kind of stuff."

"I still think a thousand is a good start," Howie said. "Say! Why don't you come in and talk to Mike? He reads the financial pages all the time."

"Nah, not tonight," I said. "I think I'll just go home and go to bed before Dad comes back. I've had enough of grown-ups for one day. Maybe tomorrow."

The next day Howie picked me up for school.

"Can you drop by this afternoon?" he asked. "I spoke to Mike and he's working at home today.

He wants to check your ideas out. He's interested, but I got to warn you, he also likes the idea of an investment club for kids. He's willing to buy a couple of units for me."

I began to get an anxious feeling in the pit of my stomach. Here I had this terrific idea, and everybody was jumping aboard and turning it into something else. They were contaminating my dream, that's what they were doing.

Now a lot of kids would be happy having an idea that's popular and go with it. But that's not my way. I get my own ideas and act on them. Still, so far, with my own idea I hadn't been able to raise a penny, if you don't count Howie's $1.57. And with just a change in the idea, the money showed signs of pouring in. Was I missing something?

I decided I'd play along for a while. After all, what did I have to lose? There might be an angle. I find there's almost always an angle.

"Okay," I said to Howie. "I'll stop by after school."

When we got to Howie's house that afternoon, Mike was in the kitchen heating a frozen pizza.

"You guys like some?" he asked.

"Sure," we said.

While we ate, Mike started asking me questions.

"I hear you're trying to raise $10,000 and you want to use it to trade stocks," he said. "What are you going to trade?"

"Dudley, between 102 and 108," I said.

Mike got up and went over to the stack of newspapers piled in a corner. He checked through several weeks of financial pages.

"Looks possible," he said. "But you really have to stay on top of it to catch all the turns. How are you going to do that?"

"I've got a friend at Star Crossed Securities. He's watching Dudley for himself. I'm sure I can get him to do it for me."

I kept my eyes on Mike's face. I saw a cloud pass over it as he thought about what to say next.

Finally he spoke. "Maybe that will work and maybe it won't. The trouble is that the market is full of surprises and even the best of plans can go sour. That's why you shouldn't put all your eggs in one basket. You ought to invest in a couple of ideas that complement each other. Then if one goes bad, the other can still be working for you."

"Look," I said, "I'm having a hard time raising enough money for one idea, let alone two."

Mike smiled and gave me one of his winks. "You're closer to getting enough money than you think."

"How's that?"

"Howie said Julie's mother is willing to put up $1,000 for Julie—if there's an investment club for kids. And I'm willing to put up $2,000 for Howie."

Mike took a deep breath and continued. "That's $3,000 for starters. Then I'm sure, as we check around, you'll find some of the other parents will go along. Five to seven thousand should be no problem."

Mike could be right. Five to seven thousand wouldn't be a problem for an investment club, but that still didn't get $10,000 working for *me*—I mean, for *Dad.* I had to keep my priorities in mind and get him out of that cartoon-character cleaning business.

Mike was on a roll. "We don't have to buy in 100-share lots. We'll spread the risk by buying smaller amounts of several stocks. Then we'll hold on to them and, to be conservative, aim to make profits of 10 to 20 percent."

I broke in, "But that isn't enough!"

"A club shouldn't gamble," Mike said.

There was that word *gamble* again. Did all the adults in our neighborhood read the same Russian story?

I shrugged. "I don't have any money to invest anyway," I said.

"I'm sure something can be worked out," Mike said. "Since you'll be doing most of the work—ferreting out the stocks, doing research, keeping the books—the club, based on its assets, could borrow a thousand on margin to cover your share. How does 10 percent of the profits sound to you?"

"What's this margin all about?" I asked.

"Going on margin is the way one can borrow against a stock position. The stocks in the account are used as collateral for the loan."

"Collateral? Margin? I don't follow you," I said.

"Collateral is a guarantee of payment. If the stock account has $10,000 worth of stocks in it, then that $10,000 of stocks can guarantee a loan of $10,000. If we used the borrowed $10,000 to buy more stock, that's called 'going on margin.'"

"Hey, that's terrific," I said. "If we go on margin, we can have $20,000 working for us, while only putting ten thousand in cash."

"Whoa," Mike said. "Too risky. If the stocks go down, we'd have to put up more cash or stocks as collateral, and if we couldn't . . ."

"Okay, I get it. So we'd only borrow $1,000—just enough to cover my end."

I started figuring using round figures. If the club had $10,000, how much might it make in a year? Mike had said 10 to 20 percent. Let's play it safe and go with 10 percent. That would be $1,000. Now if I were to get 10 percent of that $1,000, I'd end up getting $100. Only $100. And here I'd hoped that I could raise $10,000 in order to make $15,000 a year. It wasn't worth my time—or was it?

"I don't know," I said, speaking slowly.

But I kept thinking about that *margin* Mike had mentioned. That just might be the angle I was looking for. If I could *borrow* $10,000 that way, all my troubles might be over. But how could I borrow against stocks I didn't own? I was going around in circles.

"Mike," I said, "can I let you know tomorrow?"

"Take your time," Mike answered. "It's a big decision." He gave Howie one of his famous winks.

Howie walked me home. "This is exciting," he said.

"Maybe. I don't know yet," I answered.

I didn't invite Howie in because I had things to do.

The first thing I did was to check the mail. No letter from Mom. Then I noticed that there was an envelope addressed to my father from Star Crossed Securities. I held the envelope up to the light. It looked like a bill or statement or something. Now I know what you're thinking, but you're wrong. I didn't open it. But it gave me an idea.

I went to Dad's desk and found a bunch of statements with a rubber band around them. Some were opened and some weren't. I took out one of the opened ones and looked at it. I saw a list of soap companies and some figures. In one column the statement showed exactly what my dad's account was worth.

Forty-three thousand dollars.

Forty-three thousand dollars!

With that much money in stocks, why couldn't my father stop being the caped crusader against dirt?

I already knew the answer. My father was building for our future. One brick at a time.

I could build faster than that!

I wrote down Dad's account number, put the statements away, and headed for Star Crossed Securities.

NINE

I walked up to the reception desk at Star Crossed Securities. The same woman as before was manning the telephones. This time I noticed her nameplate on a stand on the desk: VIRGINIA PARSONS.

"Hello, Mr. Whitty," she said.

"Hi," I said. "How did you remember my name?"

"I have a knack for it," she said. "That's why they have me at this desk."

The phone started ringing and she handled a few calls. Then she turned her attention back to me. "Who do you want to see today?"

"Mr. Balzac, if he's not too busy."

"He's almost always busy, but I'm sure he'll work you in. Let me check."

She flicked a switch. "Jeff Whitty is here to see you, Mr. Balzac," she said. She listened a moment and then said, "I'll send him right in."

She smiled at me. "He'll see you now. Do you think you can find your way?"

"Sure," I said. "Thanks, Ms. Parsons."

I felt important as I walked down the aisle to Sid Balzac's office. I knew the office, and the people in the office were getting to know me.

Sid was talking on the phone and chewing pistachio nuts. He waved me in and motioned for me to sit in the empty chair next to Vinnie. Vinnie was going through a chartbook and making notes.

"Hi," I said.

"Hello, Jeff," Vinnie said.

"How do you know my name?" I asked him.

"Sid told me about you," Vinnie said. Then he turned to Sid and said, "I'm going to put a few orders in at the cage. Can I take anything up for you?"

Sid shook his head no and kept talking on the phone. He offered me his bag of pistachios. "I'm trying to cut back on my smoking and it's driving me crazy. I have to eat all the time."

He had whispered this to me while listening on the phone. Then I heard him say, "Yes, Mark, I understand. I'll be careful. I'll do it. Don't worry." Then he hung up.

"Hi, Kid," he said as he turned and looked at me.

"Hi, Sid," I said.

"That was my doctor. He wants me to stop smoking and take some time off. You don't smoke, do you?"

"Nope," I said.

"Well, don't start," he said. "It's a tough habit to break." Then he shifted gears. "What's happening?"

"I came to get some information."

"Shoot," he said.

"Dad's thinking of trading Dudley between 102 and 108. He doesn't have any spare cash, so can he do it on margin?"

"From what you tell me, that doesn't sound like him," Sid said. "How come he's interested?"

"I've been working on him," I answered. "I mean, there's been a sort of stock-market fever in our neighborhood ever since some of my buddies and I have been talking about starting an investment club."

"Now wait a minute. Your father wants to be part of an investment club?"

"Well, no. The club is for kids. And anyhow, Dad's kind of the independent type. He likes being on his own, you know. Being the boss and all of that. So he'd be doing Dudley on his own."

Sid turned to his display terminal and started typing. "You don't happen to know his account number, do you?"

Sid was suddenly all business. This was great!

I pulled out my notation and read him the number.

"Somehow I thought you might know it," Sid said as he popped a couple more pistachios into his mouth. "Here, I got it. Your father is cleared for margin and can borrow up to $20,000."

Twenty thousand dollars! It looked like I was in, with $10,000 to spare.

Vinnie walked back into the room as I asked, "When can he start?"

"Anytime," Sid said. "All he has to do is call in his order. Now let's see something." Sid swung back to his terminal. "Uh-oh. We've got a problem. It's over a year since your father made a transaction, and the broker who was handling him is no longer with us. We must have forgotten to assign his account to another broker."

"That's terrific," I said, "because I was counting on you to help us catch the turns."

Sid sighed. "Not so terrific. I've got to take some time off. Doctor's orders. The wife's orders. And the main office's orders. They can't get it through their heads that I have more fun at work than on vacation."

Sid drummed his fingers on the desk and looked up into the air. "Tell you what," he said. "I'm going to assign your father's account to one of the juniors. You met Harold Goodbody, didn't you?"

I nodded yes.

"Well, I'll let him service the account, at least until I get back. How does that strike you?"

I hesitated. "I don't know. We weren't exactly on the same beam last time. I wanted to know about Dudley and all he wanted to talk about was that mutual-funds stuff."

Sid laughed. "Harold's all right. He probably was just practicing his spiel. He knows how to take an order and execute it."

I wasn't so sure. I spoke up. "Can he keep on top of Dudley? Because that's what we had in mind."

"I don't know," Sid said. "How often do you expect him to get in touch with your father?"

I hadn't counted on anyone getting in touch with Dad. But by now you must know I have an answer for almost anything. I said, "Actually, my dad is always out on a job. We figured he'd check in with you once or twice a day. Or I would. And he has an answering machine. You can leave messages on it."

Vinnie had been standing there all this time watching the terminal and taking in the conversation. "I'm always around. He can contact me if Harold isn't free," he offered. "I've nothing but time."

So it was all set. Better than I could have hoped for.

Except for one tiny hurdle.

One little hitch.

But Howie could take care of that.

My pal Howie.

He'd do it for me.

All I needed was to get myself psyched up, and find the right time and place to ask him.

He'd say yes.

Wouldn't he?

After all, what are friends for?

TEN

I decided to push ahead with the investment club. The pay wasn't much, but I figured it would give me a good excuse to spend a lot of time at the brokerage office while I attended to my main interest, trading my father's account.

It wasn't quite as easy to raise the other $7,000 as Mike had thought. I even had to let Albie Lear in, although I knew he was going to make trouble at club meetings. Right off he tried to cut himself in on my free ride until he heard how much work I was going to have to do and maybe get only $100.

"You can keep it, sucker," he sneered.

Since we needed an adult to represent the club, Mike went with me to open our account at Star Crossed Securities.

I introduced Mike to Sid.

Mike explained his situation. "I work a lot at home and I track the market on my computer."

"Do you have an account with us?" Sid asked.

"No," Mike said. "Mine is with P. L. Jorgenson. But we want to open the club's account here, because Jeff recommended you and he's going to be the gofer for the club."

Sid laughed. "Thanks for the recommendation, Kid," he said.

He tousled my hair. I hoped this wasn't going to be a habit. My scalp felt itchy, and as I looked up at him, I wondered if his baldness could be catching. In addition to trading Dudley, I was scared I might end up having to *use* their Bald-Away.

Sid called Harold Goodbody in and introduced him to Mike.

"Jeff is starting an investment club," he told Harold, "and Mike Coin here will be the advisor. One of these days I'm afraid I'll have to take that vacation I've been ducking. So I'd like you to backstop me and give these guys all the help you can. Okay?"

"Okay," Harold promised.

"And one more thing." Sid scribbled something on a piece of paper and handed it to Harold. "This is Tony Whitty's account number. It's been inactive since Dick Fayette left. Jeff tells me his father may start trading soon. If he does, the account is yours."

I wished that Sid hadn't said anything about my father's account in front of Mike. But Mike's mind was on the investment club. In fact, as Mike drove me back to his house, he talked on and on about setting up the first meeting of the club. He said I should get a list of stocks together for the members to vote on. He'd go over them with me before the meeting.

When we got to Mike's house, Howie was waiting for us. "Well? How did it go?" he asked.

"Get your bike," I said. "I'll race you to our rock at the reservoir. I want to talk to you about something."

We raced to the rock. I usually win these races, but this time I let Howie win.

Howie was sitting up on the rock and panting when I reached him. "Okay, spill it," he said. "Tell me everything."

So I did, including how he could fit into my grand scheme.

"Here's how I see it," I said. "You have a lower voice than I do. So when it comes time to give Harold, Mr. Goodbody, an order, you'll call up and pretend you're my father."

"*No* way!" Howie said. "I could never pull it off. Plus I'm sure it's against the law, and if we got caught, even Mike would be mad. This has got to be the most off-the-wall stunt you ever thought up."

But I persisted. "Lighten up. We're not talking about a crime wave. Think of it as just a prank of sorts. And I'm sure you can do it. I'll write down everything you have to say, and I'll be right beside you coaching you all the way. Then when we've made all the loot, you can brag about your part in the plan. Julie will be impressed like crazy!"

The Julie bit nailed him. I could see him thinking it over and smiling.

Howie tried to act casual. He got down off the rock and picked up a pebble. Then he skipped a stone across the water. It was a six hopper.

Howie must have taken it for a good sign, because he puffed himself up and looked pleased. "Okay," he said. "I'm in. But I sure hope you know what you're doing."

"Don't worry," I assured him. "It's a piece of cake. We'll get Harold Goodbody to help us without him knowing, and there's Vinnie, who thinks nothing of making ten thousand on a day's trade. And there's Sid, when he's around. We've got it made in the shade."

"In the shade," Howie repeated. "All right! Give me five."

I gave Howie five, and then we rode home.

My plan was perfect. Everything had fallen into place. Now all I had to do was set the wheels in motion.

ELEVEN

I dropped by Star Crossed Securities and had another meeting with Sid about the investment club. He drew up a list of fifteen stocks that were popular with other investment clubs, and five others that he thought we should consider. Then he gave me all kinds of papers to take home so I could read about the companies. Official sheets and charts and reports and analyses.

When I got home, I started to study the stuff. It was very complicated and made almost no sense to me.

At first I was depressed, but then I remembered something my dad had once said when he was working on the missile system. "When things look too complicated and impossible to do, there's usually an easier way to do it."

Well, by now you must have figured out that I'm always in favor of finding an easier way to do things. This time was no exception.

I started reading the investment literature again. I discovered that if I ignored the facts and figures and charts, and just read the summary, I could quickly get a sense of what kind of business a company was in. Then I looked to see if it had a chance of growing bigger. All the other stuff in the reports seemed to have been put there just to back up the writer's point of view.

I got out some notepaper and made a list of what I thought were the seven best choices. Then I decided to test and see if I was on the right track. I stuffed my list in my pocket, gathered up all the reports, and took them over to Mike.

"What's all that?" he asked when he saw my collection of papers.

"Twenty investment ideas from Sid," I answered.

Mike took the papers from me and started thumbing through them. "You know we can't invest in all of them."

"I know," I said. "I hoped you'd help me sort

through them. I've found seven that I like."

Mike led me downstairs to his office in the basement, pointed to a chair, and told me to sit. Then he started going through the whole stack of reports, all the while grunting and pounding on his calculator.

About an hour later he said, "That should do it. I've cut the choices down to three. Let's see what you think."

He handed me a list of three stocks. I took out my list of seven stocks. We compared them. His three were on my list of seven.

He patted me on the back. "Pretty good," he said. "How did you choose yours?"

I told him.

"Okay," he said. "How do you feel about sticking with my three?"

"Okay with me," I said.

"Great," he said. "Let's call a meeting of the investment club. We'll do it on the weekend so that parents can come if they want to, and if anyone asks, you can tell how you had twenty recommendations and how we boiled down the choices to three."

"Gotcha. Except I boiled them down to seven."

"That's what I'm coming to next. Let's go over the final three."

Mike took his calculations and showed them to me. He was pretty good at explaining what the figures and charts in the reports were all about. I got the feeling he'd been waiting years to tell this stuff to someone.

I didn't quite pick up the meaning of some terms he used, like *valuation models*, but I got to understand most of them. I particularly liked *risk reward ratio.* I liked the sound of the three *r*'s, and I've always been willing to take a risk. That's another way of saying take a chance. And who doesn't like rewards?

All in all it took two hours to discuss and understand our three finalists. No question about it. I was earning my 10 percent. I was also learning a lot about the investment business, and picking up a lot of jargon that I could use at the brokerage office and at club meetings.

As we finished my lesson, Mike was busy making a paper airplane. "Are you ready to chair the meeting?" he asked.

"Chair?"

"Yeah. You know, run the meeting and make the presentation. You're not worried, are you?"

"No way," I said. "I already know the first words I'm going to say."

"What are they?"

I tried to look serious. I cleared my throat. "Dear fellow investors," I said, "welcome to the first meeting of the Sycamore Lane Investment Club."

Mike launched his paper plane at me. "Take off," he said.

I ducked. We both laughed. Then I picked up all the papers and took them home.

TWELVE

The first meeting of the investment club was held in Julie Samson's family room. Including myself, we had twelve members. At the last moment Julie had gotten a couple of her girlfriends to join. I hadn't needed Albie Lear after all, but it was too late to keep him out. We'd deposited his father's check and given him a receipt.

Mrs. Samson had set up the room so that there was a card table at one end near the fireplace. I sat at the table facing a group of folding chairs. Mike sat to my right. The folding chairs were arranged in two sections. The first two rows were straight, and the kids sat in those. The rest of the chairs were set up in an arc a little way behind the two rows. The parents who came sat in those.

Mike called the meeting to order. "The first thing we have to do is elect a president. A term of office should be six months, and then we can review how things are going. Since Jeff has sort of put this club together and has done a lot of research, I think we should elect him president."

"Wait!" said Albie Lear. "I want to be president."

"You can't nominate yourself," Mike said. "Do I hear a nomination for Albie Lear?"

No one said anything.

"If there are no more nominations," Mike said, "I suggest we vote."

At that point Albie gave Daryl Conway a big poke in the ribs. "Ouch!" Daryl said.

Albie whispered in Daryl's ear. Then Daryl stood up and said, "I nominate Albie."

"Does anyone second the nomination?" Mike asked.

"I do," said Albie.

"You can't second your own nomination," said Mike. "Does anyone want to second Albie's nomination?"

Albie looked around the room. No one seconded Albie's nomination.

Albie's father looked embarrassed. I felt sorry for him, but then I would have felt sorry for anyone related to Albie. I also felt sorry for myself, because I had to go to school with him.

"No seconds?" Mike said. "Then let's go on with the voting."

"Wait a minute!" Albie shouted. "Whitty hasn't been seconded."

"I second Jeff," said Daryl. That earned him another poke in the ribs from Albie.

Mike called for a vote, and I was elected with one vote against.

Then we elected the treasurer. Albie tried for that, but Howie won.

Then Mike suggested Albie for secretary.

"Nuts," Albie said. "I don't want to do all that writing."

Julie got the job. I could see her mother was happy.

"I now turn the meeting over to Jeff Whitty," Mike said.

"Welcome to the first meeting of the Sycamore Lane Investment Club," I said. "The management of your club has been very busy getting the club off to a good start. We've collected your money. We've opened a savings account at City Savings and an investment account at Star Crossed Securities.

"We started with a list of twenty possible investment opportunities, and we've cut that number down to three. Julie has handouts ready. They're organized in order of your management's preference. Please study them, and at our meeting next week we'll vote on buying them. Mrs. Samson says there's refreshments in the kitchen. If you have any questions, Mike Coin and I are ready to answer them. Now if there isn't any other business, this meeting is adjourned."

"Wait," said Albie. "I think we ought to invest in Pizza Planet. I like their pizzas best."

I looked at Mike and then at Julie's mother. Julie's mother was frowning. I guessed she didn't like Pizza Planet's pizza, or she didn't like Albie. Whichever, I didn't blame her.

"We'll take that up at the next meeting," I said. "Is there any other business? No? Then this meeting is adjourned."

The boys rushed to the kitchen for the goodies. The girls gathered in a corner and whispered and giggled.

Mike and I stayed at the table in case anyone wanted to talk to us and go over our reference materials. Albie's and Daryl's fathers came over.

"How did you make the stock selections?" Mr. Conway asked.

I answered first. "We got a list of stocks that other investment clubs have liked plus some that Star Crossed Securities are high on right now. After I read up on them, I picked seven as maybe being the best. Then I went to Mike here and gave him the whole original list. After he analyzed all the stocks, he made a list of his three top choices. Then we compared lists. His top three were on my list. We kept those three."

"What if someone comes up with a better idea?" Albie's father asked. "I'd like Albie to find a stock."

All I could think of was Albie's Pizza Planet, and I could hear my stomach groan.

"That would be super," Mike said. "We want everybody to think and to vote intelligently. We just started things off this way in order to show the kids how to go about it. If Albie comes up with a good stock, terrific. Let him get his facts and figures together as we've done in the handouts, and he can make a presentation at a club meeting. If the club likes his stock, then we'll vote to invest in his choice."

"That seems fair," said Daryl's father.

Mr. Lear didn't say anything. He only grunted as Albie came along and handed him a cup of cider.

Mr. Lear put his arm around Albie's shoulder and steered him down the other end of the room. I heard him say as they walked away, "Here's what I want you to do . . ."

For a minute I wondered if the reason Albie was such a wise guy was that his father was always pushing him, but then I forgot about it because Alicia Turner brought me a cinnamon doughnut and a cup of cocoa.

THIRTEEN

Over the weekend I drilled Howie on how to place orders at Star Crossed Securities. I had written a script for the first order. I even had him practice by calling me up on the phone.

On Monday afternoon I took Howie with me to Star Crossed Securities. I figured that if he saw the place, he'd feel more comfortable about phoning in the orders for my father's account. I showed him the receptionist, I pointed out Harold Goodbody, and I introduced him to Sid.

"Meet Howie Coin," I said to Sid. "He's the treasurer of our investment club."

Sid said, "I'm sure your club is going to make a lot of money, Mr. Treasurer."

Howie didn't say anything. He just sort of grinned and nodded his head. That worried me. I hadn't expected him to get tongue-tied.

Just before we left Star Crossed Securities, I checked to see where Dudley was at. The price was 103. I knew it was time to take the bull by the horns.

"Why didn't you say anything in there?" I asked Howie when we got outside.

"I just couldn't think of anything," he said.

"How are you going to do when you phone in orders?" I asked.

"Don't worry," he said. "I know that script."

"Let's find out," I said. "It's time for the first order."

"Now?"

"There's no time like now. We'll call from the store at the corner."

We found a pay phone and I handed him the number and the script.

I listened to Howie's side of the conversation.

"Mr. Goodbody, please. . . . Mr. Goodbody, this is Tony Whitty speaking. . . . Yes, he's a fine boy. Can I give you an order now? Jeff just reached me and said he noticed that Dudley was at 103.

Could you put an order in to buy 100 shares at 101½ if it goes down to that? . . . Good. Thank you. Good-bye.

"Whoowee! I did it! That was exciting!" Howie screamed. "See, you can count on me!"

We rushed home just in case Mr. Goodbody should try to reach Dad. I didn't want Dad to get a report of the purchase on the answering machine.

When we got home, we barely had time to turn off the machine when the telephone rang. I answered.

It was Harold Goodbody. "Hi, Jeff. Would you tell your father that he purchased 100 shares of Dudley at 101½ and Dudley is now trading at 105?"

"I sure will," I said.

I had picked up the stock at the low of the day, and it was now headed *up*.

I had no idea how long it would take Dudley to reach 108, but I decided to take no chances. After a twenty-minute wait I had Howie call up again and place an order to sell 100 Dudley at 107½, good till canceled. That meant the order would sit there unless I decided to cancel it.

We hung around my house until the market

closed, but we didn't get another call from Harold Goodbody.

The next morning I checked the newspaper to see where Dudley had closed. The closing price was 104¼. The high for the day had been 105⅜. That meant Dudley had moved up a little after Mr. Goodbody spoke to me. Then it had moved down, but it was still up from where I had bought it.

At school I was so excited about what was happening to Dudley that I hardly paid any attention to what was going on in class.

Howie was pretty excited too. He kept asking me, "When are you going to check in on what's going on?"

After school Howie and I rushed home to see if Mr. Goodbody had left a message on the answering machine.

He had. "Mr. Whitty, this is Harold Goodbody at Star Crossed Securities. I want to report that you sold 100 shares of Dudley at 107½. You made $600 less commissions on the trade. Dudley is now trading at 106."

"How do you like that?" I asked Howie. "We made $600 in one day and didn't have to put up a cent. Do I know what I'm doing or do I know what I'm doing?"

"I've got to hand it to you," Howie said. "Let's celebrate now that you're rich."

"*I'm* not rich. The money's my dad's. I'm doing this for him, remember?"

Howie looked disgusted. "Okay, so you've got a rich father. When does he get the money? Maybe he'd like to celebrate with us."

"Not right away," I explained. "I want to keep the money in the account for now and make it grow. That's the whole idea. I want Dad to have enough so he can stop being a Mr. Sanitary Master, and $600, less commissions, won't do it."

"What if he finds out what you're doing and thinks you're butting in where you don't belong? Doesn't Star Crossed Securities send him information on his account?"

"Sure, but Dad puts most of that stuff in the drawer without looking at it, because he thinks he's not doing any active business with them. He may not find out till next March, when he sits down with his accountant and prepares his income tax. By then we'll have made so much money, he'll be too happy to be mad!"

"He'll be mad if he has to visit us in jail," Howie said.

FOURTEEN

I left Howie shaking his head and went down to Star Crossed Securities.

When I got there, Vinnie was sitting at Sid's desk.

"Hi, where's Sid?" I asked.

"He's still at lunch," Vinnie said. "What's up?"

"I was wondering about Dudley. Dad bought some at 101½ and sold it at 107½."

"Good trade," he said. "I did it too."

"You did? Then what do you think Dad should do next?"

"I'm selling Dudley short."

"What do you mean, selling short?"

"Selling short means selling something you don't have and buying it back in at a later time. You sell when you think a stock might be heading down."

"I don't understand how you can sell something you don't own."

"Do you happen to know what buying on margin is?" Vinnie asked.

"Sure do!" I said. "My friend Mike told me all about it. You borrow money against the stock in the account and use it to buy more stocks. You can do it when there's enough stock or cash in the account for collateral."

"Good," Vinnie said. "Well, selling short is a lot like that. Except that instead of borrowing money, you borrow stock and sell it all in one step in the account. Then when you buy the stock back, it automatically is returned to the broker. The difference between what you sell it for and then buy it back for is your profit or loss."

"Can anyone do that?"

"Yes, if they have collateral in the account."

"If they're selling, why do they need collateral?"

"Because if the stock they sell goes up, they will be losing money. The broker wants protection against that kind of loss, just like he wants protection when stock is bought on margin and goes down."

"That makes sense," I said. "And that's what you're doing now? Selling short? Selling Dudley short?"

"Yes. I'm selling Dudley short at 108 and planning to buy it back at 102. That way I hope to make $600 on each 100 shares I sell."

I had a question to ask myself. Was Vinnie a genius or just lucky or both? I suspected that he was a stock-market genius. He knew how to make money and keep on making it. This seemed to be his whole life, although Sid had told me there were two ladies named Maria and Blanche who baked cookies and knitted socks for him and wanted to marry him. But they didn't hang around Star Crossed Securities.

I made a decision. I would follow Vinnie. Wherever he went, I'd be his shadow.

I had to get in touch with Howie immediately. I ran to his house.

FIFTEEN

"You and I are selling short," I said to Howie. "It's a way to trade in the stock market, but instead of saying you want to buy 100 Dudley at 108 you say you want to sell short 100 at 108. See, we're hoping it goes down to 102, and we'll buy it there and make $600."

"I don't understand," said Howie.

"All you have to do is say the right words over the telephone. Understanding what you're saying is not a requirement."

"Staying out of jail is a requirement," Howie said.

"Please . . ."

Howie was an absolute robot when he put in the order to sell Dudley short. It worked out well, being a robot. He didn't stumble, he didn't hesitate, and, best of all, he didn't think.

But suddenly *I* became a basket case. The next day at school I couldn't think about anything except shorts, the short, or whatever. It gets confusing when you've been hoping a stock will go up and then you hope the opposite. Up, down, what will it be? Should I have stayed with hoping *up*? What if I was losing my father's money?

"Are you ill, Jeff?"

Ms. Kelly was talking to me.

"The expression on your face is . . . well, you don't have a fever, do you?"

"No, I was just thinking about my father. I mean . . ."

"Oh, that reminds me," said Ms. Kelly, "I haven't heard from him. Has he decided about Career Day? I'd like an answer very soon."

"He's awfully booked up," I said. "But I'll let you know."

I spent the rest of the week hanging around Star Crossed Securities in my spare time, quizzing Vinnie.

"That Dudley short you told me about . . . I can't figure out from the newspaper exactly what's going on."

"That's because you didn't stop to get an education on selling short," Vinnie said. "The situation's A-okay. It's just taking longer than usual. Short was definitely the way to go."

Way to go. *Way to go!* Yeah!

SIXTEEN

On Friday night we held the second meeting of the Sycamore Lane Investment Club. The meeting went so smoothly, I couldn't believe it. Everyone voted for the three stocks Mike and I had picked.

"I'll phone in the orders on Monday," Mike said. "And now let's adjourn and enjoy the refreshments."

"Boy, that was easy," I said to Mike as I munched on a chocolate chip cookie.

Mike gave me one of his winks, and that was that.

I kind of liked the club. It seemed peaceful

compared to the roller-coaster ride I was on with Dudley.

But one day the ride was over. In the middle of the next week Dudley got down to 102. Vinnie got out, so I did too.

I had made another $600. At this point I was ahead of the game by $1,200!

Now I had to find out what Vinnie was doing next.

I went down to Star Crossed Securities. Sid was there, but no sign of Vinnie.

"Looking for Vinnie?" Sid asked.

He had noticed that I had sort of been trailing Vinnie lately. But between watching his monitor, eating his pistachio nuts, talking to clients, and taking a few days off here and there, Sid had his head into other things. Besides, I think he got a kick out of seeing an old man and a young kid become buddies.

A couple of days later, Vinnie showed up. "I almost got married," he explained. He didn't say whether it was to Maria or Blanche.

"I decided it wouldn't have been a good transaction," he chuckled.

"What are you going to do about Dudley now?" I asked.

"I'm finished with Dudley."

"Finished? That's like saying good-bye to an old friend," I said.

"That's the way it is. I'm looking for something else to invest in."

"Like what?" I asked.

"Like publishing giants, or food chains, or computer companies."

I listened. I really listened.

In the next three weeks I followed Vinnie in and out of three different stocks. One of the trades was a short. At the end of that time Dad's account had grown by an unbelievable $15,000. Fifteen thousand dollars!

Only Howie, who had been calling in my orders, knew what I'd pulled off, and it really blew his mind. We were in my house going over the figures. "Let's tell your father," he said. "It's time."

"No way," I said. "We're just getting started."

"Well, count me out!" Howie said. "This is getting too big for me."

It's funny how things affect different people in different ways. While I was getting more confident with every trade, Howie was getting more nervous.

Howie continued, "One of these days your father will find out. Then he'll tell Mike, and

Mike will have my hide. I like my relationship with Mike and I sure don't want to risk it just because you're greedy."

"Greedy? I'm not greedy, I'm just realistic. My dad needs more than fifteen thousand dollars to stop being the masked crusader against dirt."

"Well, he'll have to do it without me, because I'm getting out of the pretending-to-be-your-father business unless I get written permission from him and Mike."

"Ha, ha," I said.

"Let's drop it," Howie said. "What did you get for the answer to number nine on the math homework?"

SEVENTEEN

We all know what the word *crash* means, right? Wrong. My friends think a crash is what happens when a pizza pan drops. Or a shelf gets overloaded with baseball gear and collapses. Or when two bikes collide. That's what I used to think, until I got into the stock market. In the stock market, *crash* is the ugliest word invented.

In the stock market, crash means you can lose your shirt, which is just an expression. Actually you can lose everything you invested in the market. And if you happened to have invested everything in the market, well, *good-bye everything!*

A few days after my traumatic conversation with Howie, I decided to go sniffing at Star Crossed Securities to see what was new.

Sid and Vinnie were sitting quietly in Sid's office looking alternately at the monitor and staring off into space. I could tell from their expressions that not much was going on.

"What's good today?" I asked.

Sid shrugged. "Maybe lunch," he said.

I looked at Vinnie, who seemed deflated.

"Nothing," he said.

"What do you mean, nothing? There's got to be something."

"The whole market is priced too high," Vinnie said. "I'm worried. The market could drop like *that.* Down, down, down, crash!"

"But you don't have anything to worry about," I said. "You're not invested right now, are you? You're out of Dudley and the publishing companies, the food chains, the computer companies. You're all in cash."

"You're alert, Jeff," Vinnie said.

I was more than alert. I was Vinnie's shadow. I had been doing whatever Vinnie had been doing. So *I* didn't have any investments right now either. I was sitting with a cash profit of $15,000 in my dad's account. A crash couldn't hurt me.

But then I remembered the investment club.

"The investment club!" I said.

I turned to Sid. "Maybe Vinnie could be wrong about the market this time?"

"I don't know, Kid," Sid said. "I don't see it the way he does, but I've also learned not to bet against him. He's just too good."

"Should we sell the investment club account?" I asked.

"I'd sell everything," said Vinnie.

"Even my father's soaps?"

"Everything!"

"Let's look at the club's account, Kid," Sid said. "It's up 30 percent already. If you sell everything and come back, you'll have a lot of extra commissions. On the other hand, you do have a 30 percent profit in a very short period of time. It's more than you were expecting in a year. It wouldn't be surprising if stocks that moved up so fast pulled back for a while. However, investment clubs don't usually go in and out. Why don't you check with your members?"

I decided to do just that. I headed for Howie's house. I hoped Mike was home. He and Howie were in the kitchen.

I reported on what Vinnie and Sid had said. I asked Mike, "What do you think? Should we sell?"

"Maybe we should," he replied. "We'll call an

emergency meeting of the club for tomorrow night."

Howie called the boys, and I called Julie. Julie said she'd call the other girls.

The only trouble we had at the meeting was with Albie. He said, "I'll only vote to sell all the stocks if we can buy some Pizza Planet. It's my turn to pick a stock."

The club voted to take our profits and not to buy Pizza Planet.

Mike tried to appease Albie. "Maybe later," he told him.

The next day we placed an order to sell all the stocks at whatever price they were at when the market opened.

The market opened higher and we got an extra $500.

The market continued up the next day.

What was going on here? Where was the crash? It wasn't happening.

That evening Mike got a number of angry calls from the parents of some of the members.

Daryl Conway's father said, "I thought the club was in for the long haul. Selling after only a few weeks doesn't sound like the long haul to me."

Mike was mad. "Were you asleep at the

meeting? We all voted, remember?"

"Actually I may have nodded off," Mr. Conway said.

"Look," Mike said, "things looked too overheated to us, so we figured it was better to be safe than sorry. We can always go back in. I personally think we'll get a better opportunity in a few weeks."

Mr. Conway grunted and hung up.

Then Mr. Lear called. "I missed your emergency meeting," he said, "but Albie told me what you've done. He also said you voted against him again. I don't think that's fair. I want to take my money out of the club."

"That's your privilege," Mike told him, "but if I were you, I'd be patient. Maybe next time we'll vote on Albie's idea, if he makes a complete presentation."

"Well, I'll give you one week," Mr. Lear said grudgingly.

After Mr. Lear hung up, Mike said to me, "Parents! They're worse than kids."

The next day we were vindicated. The market sold off a whopping 22 percent. No one pulled their money out of the club.

Mr. Conway rang Mike up. "Good call on the market. You guys wouldn't want to manage all my money, would you?"

We didn't hear again from Albie's father.

Apparently the word got out how well we'd done, and a couple of other kids asked me if they could join the club.

The investment club was safe. I felt good about that, especially when the market continued to go down.

But my joy didn't last long. I had forgotten something. My father's soap stocks! I checked on them. They were down just a little. Slowly slipping in their own suds, you might say.

But I felt they were headed for disaster. Maybe *I* could just sell his soap stocks for him before total disaster struck.

No. Dad believed in those stocks. It had to be *his* decision.

I picked breakfast time to talk to Dad.

"Dad," I said over my cereal, "the stock market is going down. The investment club sold out all their stuff. I think you should sell your soap stocks before they go down anymore and . . ."

He didn't let me finish.

"Jeff, those companies are good long-term investments, and I'm in them for the long haul. I don't care if the market goes up or down."

"But . . ."

"No buts."

And that was that. I didn't dare sell my father's beloved soap stocks, since he cared so much about them.

But it wasn't fair. Here he was going to be losing money while I was making it. He was costing me my chance to stop being the son of San.

There was only one thing I could do, and that was to try harder. I had to make back what he was losing in his soaps.

EIGHTEEN

I kept hounding Vinnie on his next move.

He kept saying, "Wait."

Then one day I noticed he was putting in orders.

"What are you buying?" I asked.

"Wheat futures contracts," he said.

"How come?" I asked.

"Because I hear there's a wheat shortage in Russia and I believe they'll have to buy from us."

"Is this anything for my dad?"

"I doubt it," he said. "I can afford the risk, but maybe he can't. The rewards can be huge, but he could lose more than his whole investment."

"What exactly is a wheat futures contract?" I asked. "Is it anything like a stock?"

"Not really. It's a commodity. It's only like a stock in that you can trade it through a stockbroker."

"What's the difference, then?"

"As you know, a share of stock is a part interest in a going business. As long as its company is in business, the stock has some value and can hope to gain more value as the years go by and the business improves. Are you with me?"

I nodded. "So far. Go on."

Vinnie continued. "A commodity, such as wheat, has nothing to do with earnings past, present, or future. It's a pure case of supply and demand. If there's a lot of wheat around, the price will be low. If there isn't enough wheat around to meet demand, the price will be high. Right now the price is low, but if the Russians need to buy wheat, that should push its price higher in a very short time. They'll need a lot of wheat and they'll need the wheat *soon,* because they have to eat it soon and not next year. The futures contract gives me the right to buy wheat at today's low price. If wheat goes up, then I'll be able to sell the contract for the wheat at a higher price, and I expect to be able to do that soon."

Buy low, sell high. That sounded good to me. I made up my mind. If my dad had bet his life on the cleaning business and soaps, why shouldn't I place a small bet on wheat? We always buy wheat in one form or another, so what's a little bit more? Good old basic whole grain wheat—cereal, bread, muffins—solid stuff. This felt right . . . *wholesome!* And I wasn't alone. Vinnie was with me, and if he was right, then the Russians would be with me, too.

I went to get Howie to call in an order for a wheat contract.

"Howie, old friend, I've got a favor to ask you," I said.

"Anything, old friend," he said, "as long as it doesn't have something to do with calling orders in to Star Crossed Securities. It has made me too jumpy. I can't do it anymore."

"What if I pay for a date with Julie?" I asked.

"A no is a *no*!" Howie said.

I could tell he meant it.

As I left Howie, I knew that if I was going to buy wheat, I was going to have to place the order myself! And I'd have to do it by imitating Howie imitating my dad.

When I got home, I checked the entire house

to make sure no one else was there. This was no time to get caught in the act. As I started to dial Star Crossed Securities, I felt so nervous that my hand shook and I was afraid my voice wouldn't get out of my throat.

When Ginnie answered "Star Crossed Securities," I said, "H-harold Goodbody, please."

She put me right through.

I heard a click and then a voice said, "Harold Goodbody."

Before I could catch myself, I answered, "Hello . . . this is my father speaking."

There were a couple of seconds of silence. Then, "Who's this?"

I recovered and said, "This is Jeff Whitty's father."

Harold Goodbody said, "Haven't heard from you since the crash. How have you been?"

"Busy," I said. "I'd like to order a wheat contract. Can you do that?"

"Can do," Harold replied. "It's currently at $3.20 a bushel. Do you want one 5,000 bushel contract?"

"That would be $16,000!" I said.

"Yes, but you can buy it on margin with only $1,800 down."

"Do it. Buy one contract at the market," I said.

"Which month do you want?"

Month? This was a new wrinkle. Vinnie hadn't said anything about months. I had the uneasy feeling that I didn't know enough about what I was doing, but I plunged ahead.

"I'll take the soon month."

"The soon month?" Harold seemed puzzled. "Do you mean the nearby month? That would be May."

"Yeah," I said. "That would be it. Buy me one May wheat."

Then I hung up.

C'mon, wheat!

NINETEEN

My days of working with Howie were over. Maybe it was just as well. If he was afraid of placing one more order before, he would have been terrified at what I did next. When I think about it, I'm terrified at what I did next.

Wheat started moving up. I kept picking Vinnie's brains about the wheat futures market. I already knew that I could buy one wheat contract with only $1,800 down, hardly anything at all. Now I learned that if the contract went up in price, I could, without putting up any more money, add more contracts based on the increased value in the account.

So here's what I did. When May wheat was at $3.35, I bought two more contracts. That gave me three contracts at an average price of $3.30.

That meant I had a total investment of $5,400 in wheat, and thanks to margin, that $5,400 was controlling wheat costing $49,500. I figured that $5,400 was a safe amount to risk, in case the wheat market dipped, because I still had the nice cushion of a $15,000 cash credit in the account.

Where did the $15,000 come from? In case you forgot, it was the profit resulting from my stock-market trades.

Wheat kept going up! I began paying attention to weather reports from around the world. There was a drought in Russia and China.

Vinnie kept chanting, "Rain, rain stay away."

I kept repeating, "The Russians are coming."

Wheat hit a price of $3.66.

"How far can wheat go?" I asked Vinnie.

"At least to $5.00," he said.

I placed an order for another three contracts. Wheat kept on rising and I kept on buying!

In the middle of April, wheat reached a price of $4.74. Here's how my father's account looked at that time:

18 wheat contracts, net worth:	$97,200
Unused wheat margin:	4,000
Cash in the account:	15,000
Total:	$116,200

And that didn't count the soap stocks.

I was trying to decide what to do next. As it turned out, I had to decide *fast.* A long weekend was coming up at the end of the month thanks to teachers' clerical day, which meant a day off from school. Mom thought it'd be nice if Dad and I joined her at Grandma's. Grandma was feeling better, but Mom still didn't want to leave her. Dad said that his foreman could take care of the cleaning business for a week.

After talking back and forth, this was the plan. Dad and I would leave on the morning of Friday, April 30, and return home Wednesday, May 5. Dad said it was okay for me to miss a couple or so days of school.

I had to make some important decisions before I took off and lost touch with Star Crossed Securities. So on Monday, April 26, I sold twelve of my eighteen contracts and nailed down a $60,000 profit. I now had more than $115,000 in stocks and credits in Dad's account in case anything went wrong with the six contracts still working for me.

I was a little surprised at myself, but the minute Harold confirmed the sale of the twelve contracts, I had a great sense of relief. I guess I'd been going overboard in the market. I found I was actually looking forward to going to Grandma's.

Before we left on Friday, I checked the newspaper. The Russians had come into the market and wheat was really jumping. When I had sold the twelve contracts, it was like leaving a party too soon. Like leaving before the guest of honor arrived. I made some quick calculations. I figured that Dad's account was now worth $145,000! If I hadn't sold, it would have been worth a lot, lot more. But at least I had the remaining six contracts working for us.

At Grandma's things were pretty dull, but Dad enjoyed the break in his routine. He slept for nine hours the first night, something he couldn't do at home. And he spent hours sitting on the back porch reading books and newspapers.

I tried reading to Grandma, but she kept falling asleep.

Then I tried helping in the kitchen, but Mom shooed me out. I watched TV, but I soon got bored with that. Then I started picking on Terri.

I must have been getting on Mom's nerves, because on Sunday she said, "Why do you keep pacing back and forth, Jeff? You're making me nervous."

"I have nothing to do," I told her. "And I can't remember if I locked the door when we left. I just know that we forgot to water your collection of prize spider plants, and I'm sure we forgot to turn on the answering machine."

The thirsty spider plants got her. "Tony," she said to my dad. "Maybe you ought to take Jeff home and water my plants."

But Dad wasn't ready to leave. So it was arranged that I'd go home alone on Monday and stay with Howie, and I was given the big job of saving the plants.

"I'll be home in two days," Dad said.

"Don't worry, I'll take care of everything," I promised as I got on the bus.

TWENTY

That evening, back home, Howie and Mike met me at the bus stop.

"Hello, Mr. President. Long time no see," Mike said as I got off the bus.

"We'll have a lot of fun with you bunking at our house," Howie said.

"Yeah," I said.

I didn't say much as we drove home to Sycamore Lane. I hadn't realized it before, but ever since Howie had stopped calling Star Crossed Securities for me, we had drifted apart. I'd been living in another world, the world of high finance. I had wanted to take Howie with me into that world, but he didn't want to come.

As I sat there in the backseat of the car, I looked at Howie's enthusiastic face, and it struck me how much I had missed him. How I was letting an important part of my life slip away. I promised myself that I'd have to do something about that. After all, a best friend, one you can really care about, is hard to come by.

I nudged Howie. "Hey, remember there was something you wanted me to do but I didn't want to do it? Well, now I do."

Howie knew what I was talking about. "It has something to do with the number *fifteen*, right?"

"Right," I said.

Howie didn't know that the $15,000 had grown at last count to $145,000. He didn't know that I had taken over his job of pretending to be my father. This wasn't the time to tell him. First I had to tell my father.

There was enough money now for Dad to take his profits and change his life. That is, if he wanted to. Hey, whatever happened to my plan to banish Mr. Sanitary Master? To get him out of my father's life and mine? Somewhere along the way, that cartoon character had become smaller and smaller in my head. Maybe it was because other things had become bigger. Like getting involved in the stock market. Or maybe it was just dawning on me that some decisions belong to other people and not to me.

In any case I no longer cared about my father being a cartoon character. I could live with it. I could even ask Dad to go to Career Day, T-shirt and all. All I really wanted to do was to be a kid again and hang out with Howie, go to school, play ball, and not go to jail.

Suddenly I could hardly wait for Dad to come home so I could tell him how rich I had made him and how sorry I was about how and why I did it.

Should I tell him first about rich or first about sorry? I went with rich.

When we got to Sycamore Lane, I dropped my bag off at Howie's and then went over to my house.

We have a mail slot in our front door. When I opened the door, I found the foyer littered with mail.

I picked up the mail and thumbed through it. I wanted to intercept anything from Star Crossed Securities and stick it in Dad's drawer. Dad would probably stick it in there anyway. But I had to make sure that I had a chance to talk to him first, just in case he decided to open something.

The usual confirmations and statements were

there. But there was something else. A card for my father from the postal service stating that they had tried to deliver a registered letter, but since nobody was home they couldn't leave it. It had to be picked up at the local branch post office. I don't know why, but I got a strange feeling in the pit of my stomach.

It was Monday evening and the post office was closed till the morning, so I worried about the card all night on Howie's lumpy guest cot and through the next day at school.

When I got to the post office, Mr. Samuels was on the desk. He knows me. He used to be on our route. I gave him the notification card and asked him for the registered letter. He had me sign a form and gave me the letter. It *was* from Star Crossed Securities.

I went outside and opened the letter. It was very official, and read:

> *Dear Mr. Whitty:*
>
> *You are hereby notified that your contracts for wheat became due and the rights therein were assigned. Since we were unable to reach you, we liquidated and used the assets in your account to meet your obligations under the rules of the exchange.*
>
> *Currently 30,000 bushels of wheat are being*

shipped to you. Contact us before 1:00 P.M. *on May 3 if you want the wheat delivered anywhere other than to your registered address . . .*

The rest of the letter was some legal stuff that I didn't understand.

I was in a panic. What had I done? Did this mean we were broke? What could I do?

I needed help!

I needed Sid.

I ran home to call him.

TWENTY-ONE

I dialed Star Crossed Securities.

Ginnie answered.

"It's Jeff Whitty," I said. "Give me Sid and hurry! It's an emergency!"

"Sorry," she said. "Sid's finally on vacation, Jeff. Isn't that terrific? He really needs it."

I could have told her what would have been really terrific, but I just asked to be put through to Harold Goodbody.

"Harold's line is busy. Can I have him call you?" Ginnie offered. "Are you at home?"

"Yes," I said. "Tell *him* it's an emergency."

I thought about calling Vinnie, but I didn't want to tie up the line in case Harold Goodbody tried to return my call.

Why does it always seem so hard to get ahold of someone when you really need him? I must have walked up and down the house fifty times before the phone rang.

I rushed to the phone. "Hello," I said.

"This is Harold Goodbody. Is that you, Jeff?" the voice on the line said. "What's the emergency?"

"What's the *emergency*? How can you ask that? We got this registered letter with a bunch of words I don't understand except the part that says 30,000 bushels of wheat are being shipped to our house."

"I know. I got a notice on Friday that the contracts had been assigned and exercised. I tried to reach your father to see what he wanted to do, but nobody answered, not even the answering machine."

I was stunned. "But we had *May* contracts," I stammered. "Friday was *only April.*"

Harold said, "True. But Friday was the first notice day for the May wheat contract. When the first notice day comes, the contracts can be assigned anytime until after their last official trading day."

"What does that mean?"

"Simply put, your father bought some wheat contracts. The contracts came due and he didn't close them out. Now the wheat's his."

"Can't Dad own the wheat without it coming to our house?"

"Uh . . . well, I *think* so, but . . . that's more or less a *guess*," Harold said. "When it comes to commodities, I know how to write a ticket, but that's about it. Now if your father had only gone into mutual funds, I could be more helpful. They're my specialty."

Oh, great. I had two disasters. The wheat and Harold, who only knew how to write tickets.

"What about my dad's account? Is he broke?"

"Not exactly. His stocks are gone and so is most of his cash. They went to pay for all that wheat, you know. But your father's not broke. He still has $2,500 cash left in the account, and he owns a hell of a lot of *wheat*."

My poor father's soaps and cash, I thought. What's happened to all my dreams and hopes for him? What more could happen?

I was afraid to ask, but I had to know. "How's wheat doing now?" I asked.

Harold was enthusiastic. "It's at $5.50 and looks like it's going higher."

"That means . . ." I began.

"Right," Harold interrupted. "Your father's wheat is worth $165,000! And according to the notice you got, it's probably on its way to your house, even as we speak. What are you going to do with it?"

"I don't know," I said. "I'm sure Dad never expected to put 30,000 bushels in our house."

"When your father ordered the wheat, I'm sure he knew what he was doing," Harold said nervously.

I started to say, "Vinnie never said anything to me about *delivery*. I mean . . ."

"Vinnie?"

"Forget Vinnie. Are you sure you're giving this to me straight? We've got to stop delivery! Dad's out of town. He can't come home to find 30,000 bushels of wheat dumped on our front lawn. Can't you stop the delivery?"

I could hear Harold rustling some papers. Then he said, "I'm putting you on hold."

The phone went dead for about five minutes; then Harold came back on the line. "Too late," he said. "The third of May was yesterday. I called the main office, and they checked with the dealer. He has a confirmed order to ship the wheat. We don't know how he got it. My guess is somebody pushed a wrong button on a computer or something. Life is full of glitches. Anyhow, I guess the dealer's short on storage space, because he's already sent the wheat on its way. It should arrive tomorrow."

I figured Harold was the one who pushed the wrong button, but blaming him wasn't going to get me anywhere. I had a bigger problem than that. Wheat wasn't the only thing that was going to arrive tomorrow. Dad was.

TWENTY-TWO

I'm sitting on our front steps, waiting. Waiting for 30,000 bushels of wheat to be dumped on our front lawn. Waiting for Dad to get home. I wonder which will arrive first.

Here comes the wheat now. Trucks and trucks of it.

And here comes Dad in his car!

They're starting to dump wheat on our lawn. Dad is out of the car and running up to the wheat dumpers. "Stop!" he yells. "What are you doing to my lawn?"

I run up to Dad and pull him aside. "I've got

something to tell you," I say. "I bought this wheat for you. Thirty thousand bushels of it. About $165,000 worth."

Dad is stunned. I take him into the house and start to explain. "It all started with Career Day . . ."

I tell him everything, and how sorry I am that I was embarrassed he was Mr. Sanitary Master. And how I hope he doesn't mind being in a second business. Like it or not, with 30,000 bushels of wheat, he's in a new business, right?

Then I add, "We're sort of rich."

"Only as long as the wind doesn't blow," Dad grunts. I can tell he's unhappy. "I like being in the cleaning business," he says. "I don't know anything about wheat."

Then he's out the door to watch the wheat being dumped.

I see Howie and Albie running toward our house. I see Julie and Mrs. Samson come out of their house.

I can't even talk to them now.

I have to do *something*. I got Dad into this, and it's up to me to get him out.

Let's see. Vinnie said the Russians need a lot of wheat. They need it, Dad's got it.

I'll just call the president of Russia, right now,

and ask him if he wants to buy our wheat. I'll get Dad a done deal and a profit. That should make him happy.

Then I'll give him his choice. Does he want to speak to the class as a cleaning contractor or a wheat merchant? He'll be great as either one. He'll have to decide fast, though, because Career Day is next week. He ought to be able to do that. After all, he's my dad.

I pick up the phone and dial.

It's ringing.

"Operator, please get me the president of Russia. I've got a great deal for him on some wheat. Tell him this is my father speaking . . ."